S0-BED-980

SPECIAL REPORT:
The Kicker Cup

by Ricky Jefferson
illustrated by Marsha Winborn

SCHOOL PUBLISHERS

Copyright © by Harcourt, Inc.

All rights reserved. No part of this publication may be reproduced or transmitted in any form or by any means, electronic or mechanical, including photocopy, recording, or any information storage and retrieval system, without permission in writing from the publisher.

Requests for permission to make copies of any part of the work should be addressed to School Permissions and Copyrights, Harcourt, Inc., 6277 Sea Harbor Drive, Orlando, Florida 32887-6777. Fax: 407-345-2418.

HARCOURT and the Harcourt Logo are trademarks of Harcourt, Inc., registered in the United States of America and/or other jurisdictions.

Printed in China

ISBN 10: 0-15-350668-7
ISBN 13: 978-0-15-350668-0

Ordering Options
ISBN 10: 0-15-350600-8 (Grade 3 On-Level Collection)
ISBN 13: 978-0-15-350600-0 (Grade 3 On-Level Collection)
ISBN 10: 0-15-357865-3 (package of 5)
ISBN 13: 978-0-15-357865-6 (package of 5)

If you have received these materials as examination copies free of charge, Harcourt School Publishers retains title to the materials and they may not be resold. Resale of examination copies is strictly prohibited and is illegal.

Possession of this publication in print format does not entitle users to convert this publication, or any portion of it, into electronic format.

2 3 4 5 6 7 8 9 10 985 12 11 10 09 08 07

Characters

Sara	Coach Hurley	Andrew
Katie	Ms. Franklin	Tim
Luke	Tamara	

Setting: Millwood County Park

Sara: This is Sara Jones of the School News Network. Today we're reporting live from the Millwood County Youth Soccer Tournament. It's a battle for the biggest, most important trophy in the county—the Kicker Cup! Andrew Farmer is our top sports reporter. Andrew, how do things look today?

Andrew: Sara, this is as impressive an assembly of soccer talent as I've ever seen.

3

Sara: It's a competitive day to be sure. Now let's talk to the person behind all this. Liz Franklin is the president of the Youth Soccer Association. Ms. Franklin, are you surprised by how big this event has become?

Ms. Franklin: No, I'm not. Soccer is a very popular youth sport not only in Millwood. It is a part of cultures all around the world!

Andrew: How do you put together a tournament like this?

Ms. Franklin: It takes a lot of work! There are all kinds of chores. We have scouts research the teams to decide the best match-ups. Then we have to schedule the games and arrange for the use of the fields. We have to make sure we have all the resources we need. We're very lucky, though, that some of our local businesses have helped. They have donated items, such as refreshments, uniforms, and lights.

Sara: It sounds like a lot of work! We hope you have a successful day! Now let's go to our reporter in the field, Luke Greene.

Luke: Thanks, Sara. I'm with Jerry Hurley, coach of the tournament's top-rated team, the Gophers. Coach Hurley, what must your team do to win the Cup?

Coach Hurley: Well, we don't want to dismiss any of our opponents. There are a lot of great teams here. We're just hoping to survive the first round.

Luke: Can you tell us about your team?

Coach Hurley: They're hardworking, talented players. Sam Gordon is an independent, creative player who can always find a way to make a shot. Tamara Mitchell is a spectacular goalie who can stop anything.

Luke: There's a rumor that Tamara has a pair of lucky socks. Has she really worn them throughout your team's eighteen game winning streak?

Coach Hurley: Let's just say that Tamara is very special, and so are her socks.

Luke: That's the latest news from Field A. Back to you, Sara and Andrew.

Andrew: Thanks for your report, Luke. Sara, no matter what Coach Hurley says, the Gophers are favorites in this tournament.

Sara: Well, we're all just hoping for a good championship game this afternoon. We're also hoping Tamara's socks survive the day. Let's go out to Field D. Katie Morales is there with some breaking news. Katie, what's going on?

Katie: We have an interesting development, Sara. The game was stopped when someone noticed a bird sitting on one of the goals. The bird turned out to be a fake! Officials looked at the bird. They found a small video camera concealed inside! They think that someone decided to camouflage the camera in the bird in order to tape the game secretly.

Andrew: That's strange, Katie! Do you really think that is the case?

Katie: It is indeed, Andrew. This was no coincidence. It was definitely someone trying to tape secretly.

Sara: Thanks, Katie. Get back to us when you find out more. Now let's go to Tim Young. He's watching a shocking incident unfold out on Field H. Tim?

Tim: Sara, the game between the Stars and Hurricanes has come to a complete stop!

Sara: What's happening, Tim?

Tim: It all started innocently enough. Many of our viewers brought their families to the tournament, expecting a pleasant day of soccer. Unfortunately, some also brought their dogs. It appears that one dog is particularly enthusiastic about chasing soccer balls. Once he dashed out onto the field, there was no stopping the others. Dogs of all shapes and sizes ran onto the field. They're now involved in their own high-spirited game of soccer!

Andrew: What is going to happen?

Tim: Well, everyone is just trying to catch their dogs. Now let's speak with Tamara Young, the goalie of the Gophers. They just won their first-round game. Tamara, what was the secret to winning this game?

Tamara: There's no secret. We just played as well as we possibly could.

Tim: What about the next round?

Tamara: We always give it one hundred percent, Tim.

Tim: Well, if you win today, you should autograph your lucky socks. I'm sure they'll be worth something someday! Now let's go to Katie. She has news about the concealed camera.

Katie: A player's father has claimed the camera. He wanted to record the game and thought the goal would be the best place for the camera. However, he didn't want it to distract the players. That's the reason for the bird disguise.

Sara: That's good news, Katie. Well, Andrew, it's been a great start to the tournament. I can't wait to see what happens next.

Andrew: I can't either. When something does happen, though, you'll hear it from us first at School News Network!

Think Critically

1. What is the setting of this Readers' Theater?

2. Name three features of this story that help you know it is a Readers' Theater.

3. Why was the camera hidden in the bird?

4. Why does Tamara keep wearing the same socks?

5. Which character in this play is your favorite? Why?

 Science

Best Kick Ever! Think about kicking a soccer ball. Make a list of factors that can affect how far it travels. Share your ideas with the class.

School-Home Connection Find a sports article in a newspaper. Practice reading it aloud as if you were a news reporter. Then read it to a family member.

Word Count: 862